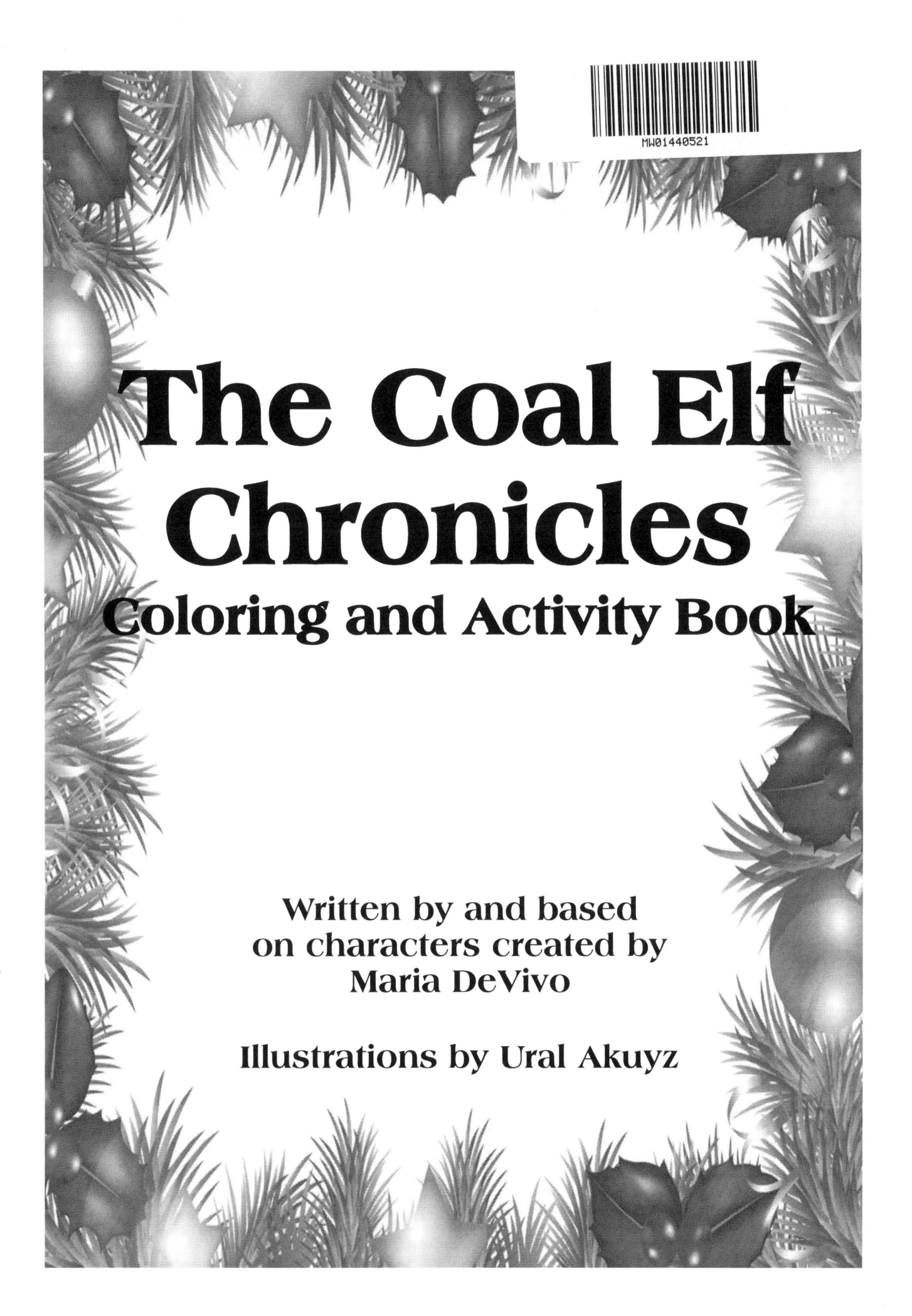

The Coal Elf Chronicles
Coloring and Activity Book

Written by and based
on characters created by
Maria DeVivo

Illustrations by Ural Akuyz

Copyright © 2019 by Maria DeVivo

All rights reserved. This book or any portion thereof
may not be reproduced or used in any manner whatsoever
without the express written permission of the publisher
except for the use of brief quotations in a book review.

Printed in the United States of America
First Printing, 2019
ISBN: 9781707674435
Imprint: Independently published

www.mariadevivo.com

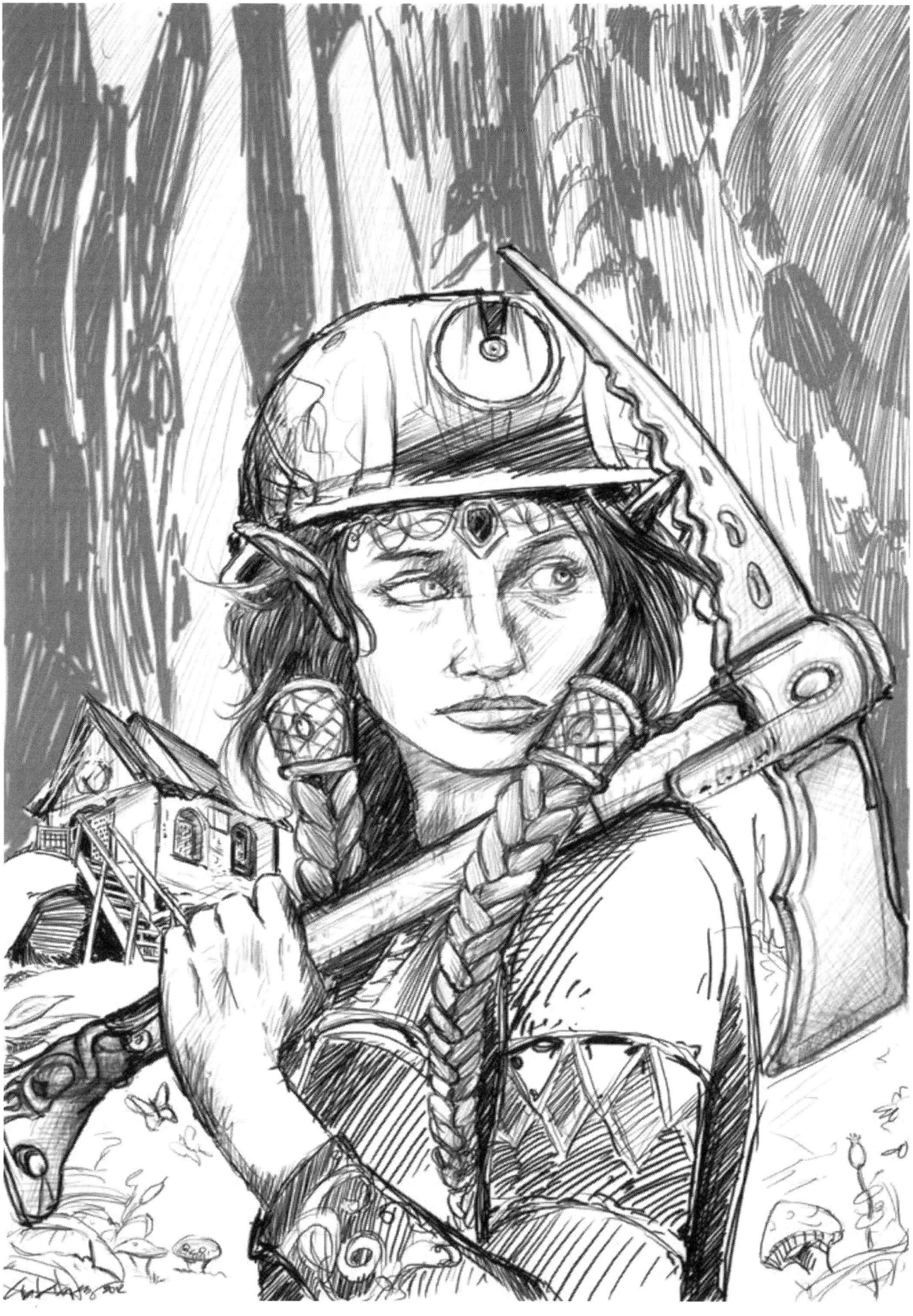

The Coal Elf
Crossword Puzzle

Across
2 Ember's adversary, wants to control the North Pole
4 Kyla's sister
7 what we celebrate
8 the Life Job Ember was assigned
9 group of elves who control much of what happens at the Pole
12 The Boss
17 a Shadow Deer, unfit for the Boss's team
18 a small, bat-like, nocturnal creature who lives in the Mines
19 The Reindeer Trainer
20 Ember's sister

Down
1 where Ember writes all her thoughts and feelings
3 The trolley car driver, Ember's crush
5 parasitic infection that Coal Elves get
6 document that determines the good and bad children for the year
10 Ember's best friend in the Mines
11 Ember's Nanny Aboveground
13 Ember's family name
14 the fruit that gauges the level of Happiness in the world
15 Ember's Master Elf, Sturd's father
16 a remedy for coppleysites

Sturd Ruprecht

NUMBERS CRUNCH!

	6	7		2	3	1		
8				9			2	7
7		5			8		9	
		9	3	6		8		2
4	7			1				3
2	6				9			1
	9	7				1		
	8		9		1	4	3	5
3	1				6	2	7	9

Help Ember and Barkuss crunch those numbers in the Mines before Banter confronts them on inconsistencies in their record keeping!

Solve the Sudoku puzzles and help Ember and Barkuss keep their secret.

		6	9	5		1	2		7
2	3	1	6		8		5		
4			7	2			1		
		4	8		2				
	9		4	1	6	8			
3			9	5	7	1			
1		2				3	9	4	
5	4			2					
9			1			5	6		

Barkuss Dwin'nae

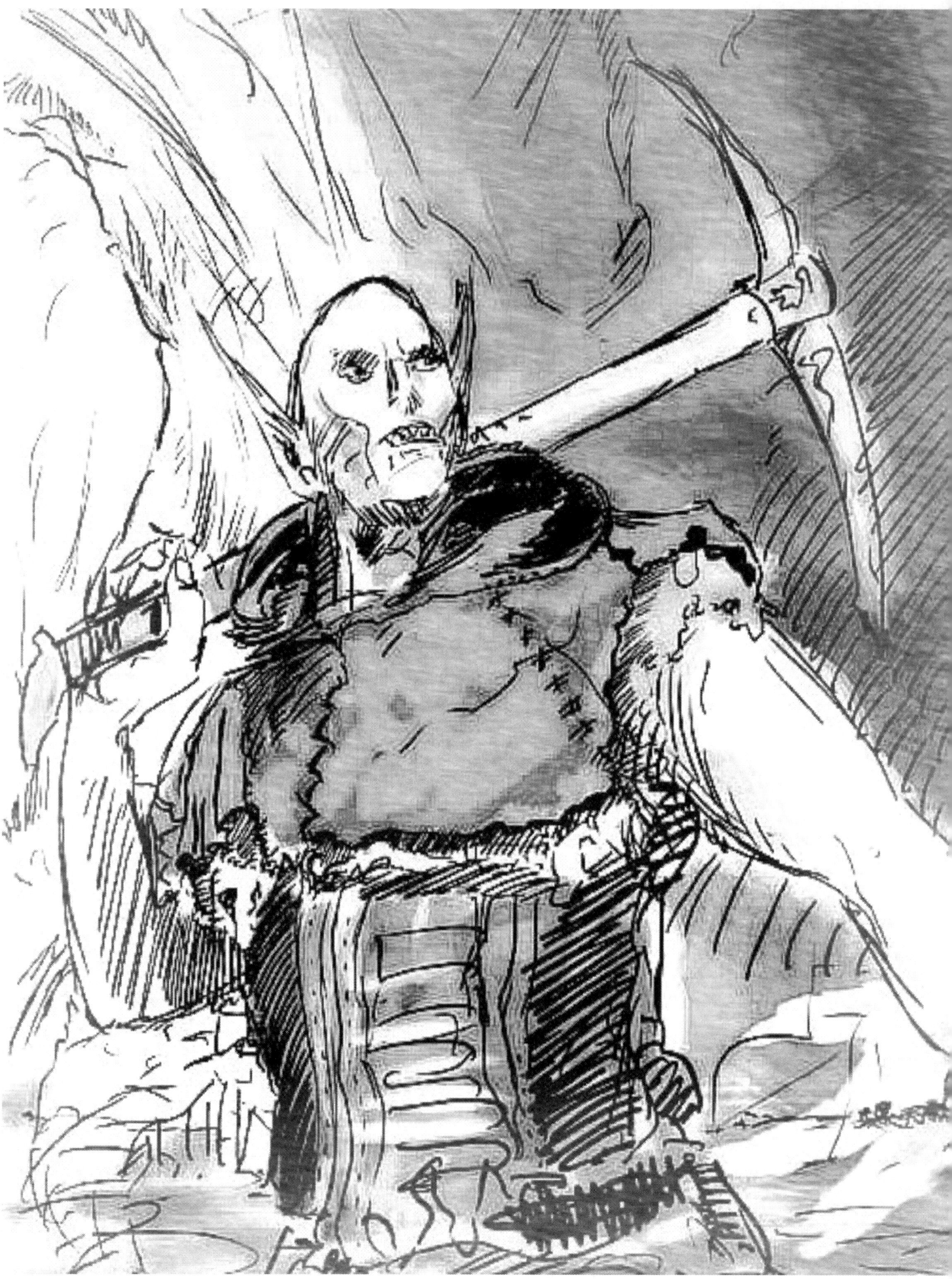

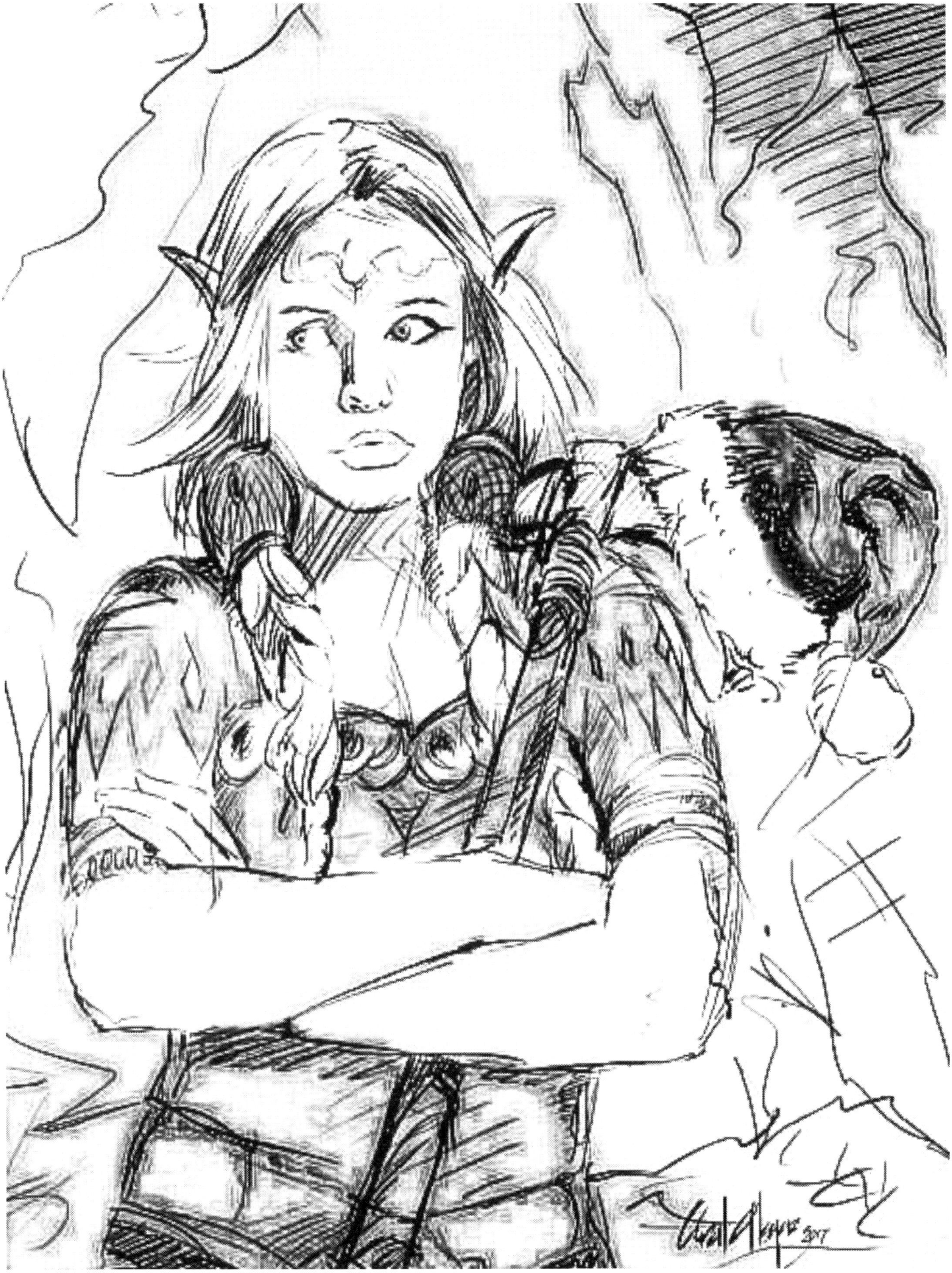

From Ember's Journal...

This time of year usually gets me all sentimental and pensive. I like to think about "constants" that have been in my life. They're like warm blankets to curl up under in my brain.

When I was younger, I hate to admit this, but my sister, Ginger, was a constant in my world. She did this thing every morning where she had to stand in front of the mirror and make this awful clicking noise with her mouth. She would only do this for a few minutes, and it grated on my every nerve, but when I left for the Mines and woke up lonely in my den, the absence of that horrific sound was worse than the sound itself.

As time passed, my new constant became my pick axe... Delilah. Yeah... I guess naming my axe kinda makes her feel friendly, and familiar. Probably stupid, right? I bet even Barkuss would laugh at me if he heard that one! But Delilah is keeps me in check, ya know? The sound as she chips away at the hard rock of the caverns is rhythmic, soothing, melodic... like a mouth making a ritualistic clicking sound in front of the mirror...

~E.S

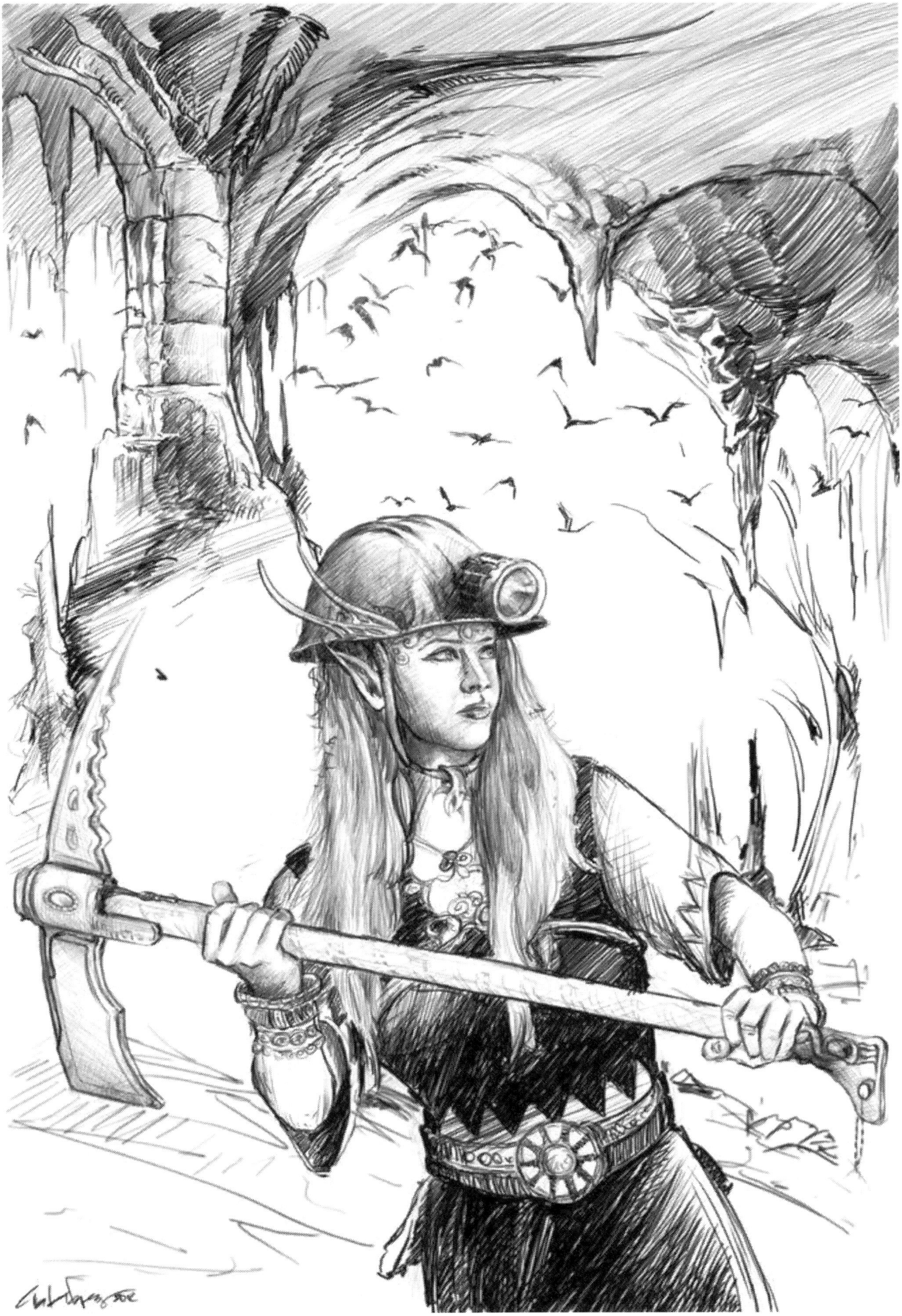

Ember wrote in her journal to get her feelings out on paper. Use the parchment to create a journal entry or a poem of your very own!

Scan the QR Code to watch the video for "Memo: Ember's Song," and follow along with the lyrics on the next page!

I can't sleep this OFF,

'Cause once is not ENOUGH.

Time goes by in a *HAZE*.

I break through the ROCK,

But I'm not BROKE!

I scream at the top of my LUNGS!

She's everything they want.

She's everything they need.

What would you do

If your world was full of coal?

With everything you know

Would you go?

I break through this ROCK,

But I'm not BROKE.

I scream at the top of my LUNGS!

She's everything they want.

She's everything they need.

She's everything...

Run From the Mines

Ember needs to make it Aboveground before Sturd and his goons find out she has the List!

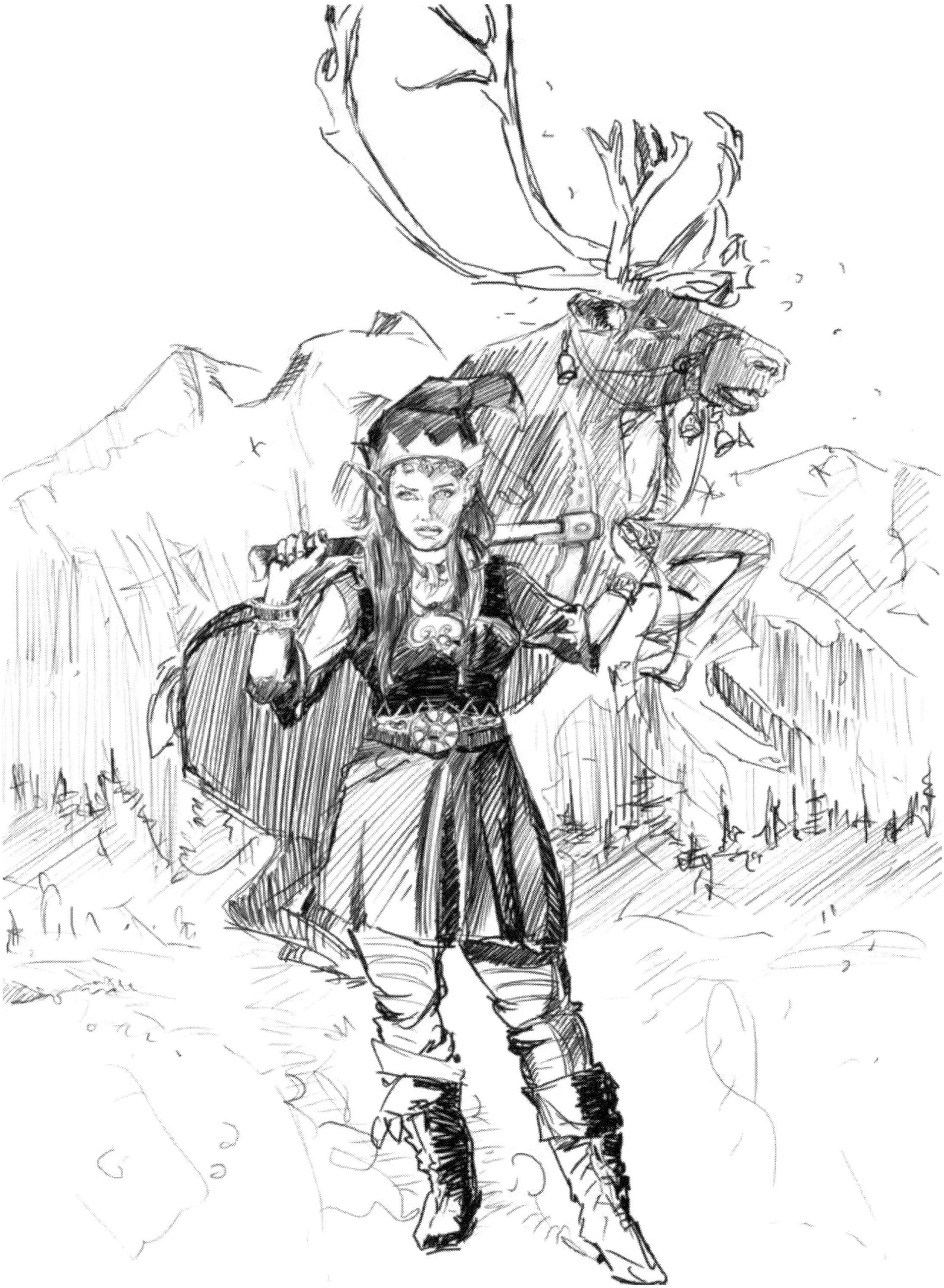

The North Pole

- Lapis Hall
- Headquarters
- Norland
- Ice Island — *Frost Weather Outpost*
- Tir-La Rise
- Tir-La Dunes — *Staxx Manor*
- Tir-La Treals — *Skye Manor*
- Brightly Stable
- West Bank — *Town Square*
- East Bank — *Town Square*
- The Inn
- Mouth of the Cave
- Plumm Stable
- Nessie Fruit Groves
- Lumber District
- Mon Valley
- Fishing District

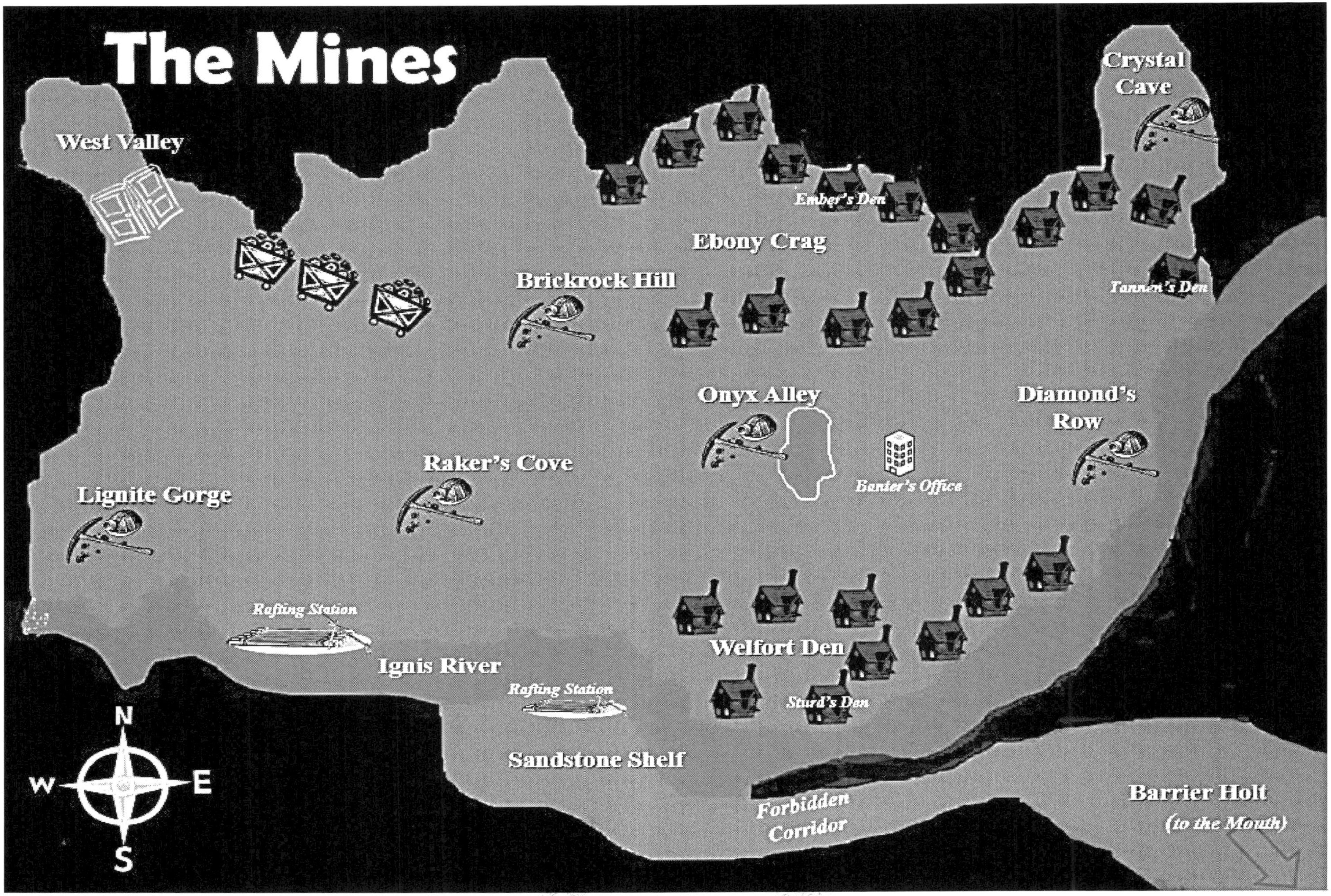

The Mines

West Valley

Lignite Gorge

Raker's Cove

Rafting Station

Ignis River

Rafting Station

Sandstone Shelf

Brickrock Hill

Ebony Crag

Ember's Den

Crystal Cave

Tannin's Den

Onyx Alley

Banter's Office

Diamond's Row

Welfort Den

Sturd's Den

Forbidden Corridor

Barrier Holt
(to the Mouth)

Official North Pole
Nice List Certificate

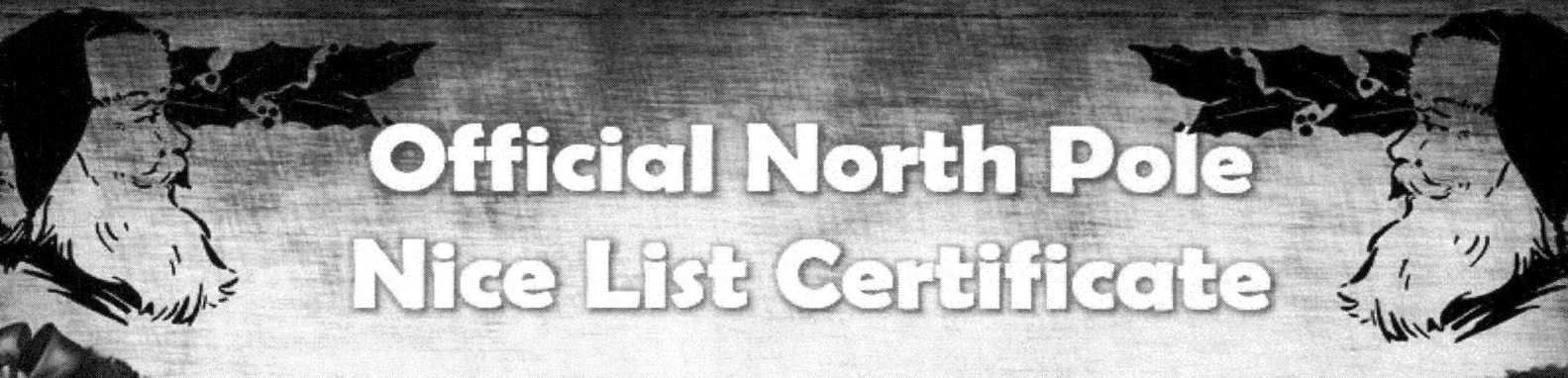

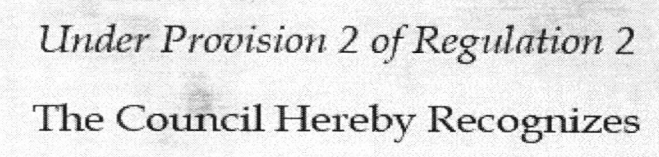

Under Provision 2 of Regulation 2

The Council Hereby Recognizes

_____

on the GOOD LIST for this year's Big Night!

Congratulations!

Ember Skye

Ember Skye, Coal Elf

www.mariadevivo.com

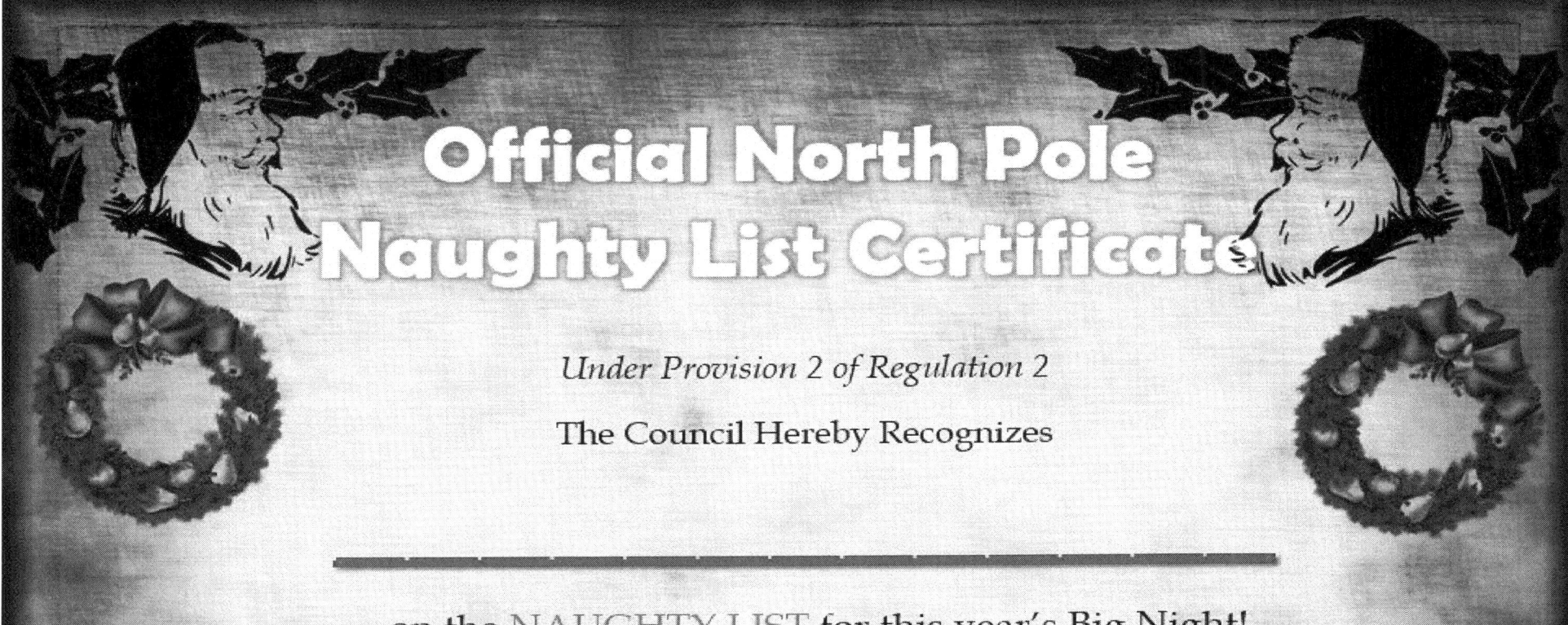

Official North Pole
Naughty List Certificate

Under Provision 2 of Regulation 2

The Council Hereby Recognizes

_____

on the NAUGHTY LIST for this year's Big Night!

DENIED

Ember Skye, Coal Elf

www.mariadevivo.com

Aboveground Life

```
U D R R J N B K Z V G J D Q F G E G B I
K N N C E W I E I V J N J I K R S O G E
M I A A K I L A M C U I S I M E I L U T
S K P A L C N Y R O D H R O F E R D S Q
L E N P O S F D R T I Z E K J N A I N N
I J L D E T I G E N E E T O K S L E B T
C S O B J R E E G E I D R O J C R Z R V
N R S V A V L D C S R A A B U A I C N M
U J F O O T I O S I F O U L D R T L O S
O U O B B S S E D A W Q Q M G F U N R K
C D A I T I N T B G P A D S J Y V H N W
M K A R O N A M I M A D A M E A A A F A
H M I B G M J E S R C S E S L P B B E C
A C L L A H S I P A L E H L J T Q B N H
T I R L A T R E A L S A E M S W S O F M
W E S T B A N K W B P Y D A D V Y G O E
F R A C S D E R A L J E E U J U R Q R Y
E A R A T N A S X I L B U D N O X B C G
V G A M D M E Y C Q S N G B V E H K E W
L J P C L P O T K M Y R J E K Z S O R K
```

ABOVEGROUND
BOSS
EASTBANK
GOLDIE
HEADQUARTERS
KIPPER
MADAME
NESSIE
STABLES
TIRLATREALS
ZELCODOR

BAYGLADETRAIN
COUNCIL
ENFORCER
GREENSCARF
ICEISLAND
LAPISHALL
MANOR
REDSCARF
TIRLADUNES
UNA

BOOK
DUBLIXSANTARAE
FISHINGDISTRICT
GROVE
INN
LIST
MONVALLEY
REINDEER
TIRLARISE
WESTBANK

Madame Claus

Mystery Message

Complete the maze to unlock the secret message in the Mines!

Answer:

_____ _____ _____

Tannen Trayth

NAME THE REINDEER!

New calves were born at the Stables, and Kyla and Fannie need help naming them. Decorate their antlers and placard for their pens, and be creative and give them names!

Kyla Plumm

He breathed in deep, closing his eyes and accepting the dirt and dust into his lungs. His body shivered when the letters of his all his emotions rearranged themselves to form his true intention in his mind. "To rule," he finally exhaled. "To rule all."
– *The Rise of Sturd* (page 55)

Sturd

EMBER

But Ember wasn't a typical elfling. Her curiosity and natural inclination to question had often landed her in trouble. Now, she was destined to be a Coal Miner? – *The Coal Elf* (page 1)

A GLIMPSE IN THE MIRROR!

Being a twin is rare – even more for the elves at the North Pole! If you were a twin, what would your other "you" look like? Would he or she be the spitting image of you (like Bambam and Juju), or would he or she be your polar opposite? Use the mirror below to design what YOUR twin would look like.

Bambam & Juju Dwin'nae

"Sturd is an engagingly detestable villain, but yet is somehow not a two-dimensional caricature. His obsession with chaos, and his desire for power are credibly rendered, but one still grits one's teeth at his actions, and hopes to see him find his comeuppance." – *Goodreads Reviewer, Michael Watson*

"As expected, this book does have hot cocoa, candy canes and lollipops, but the elven society is a sugar-coated hell..." – *M.C. O'Neill, author of The Angels and the Ancients*

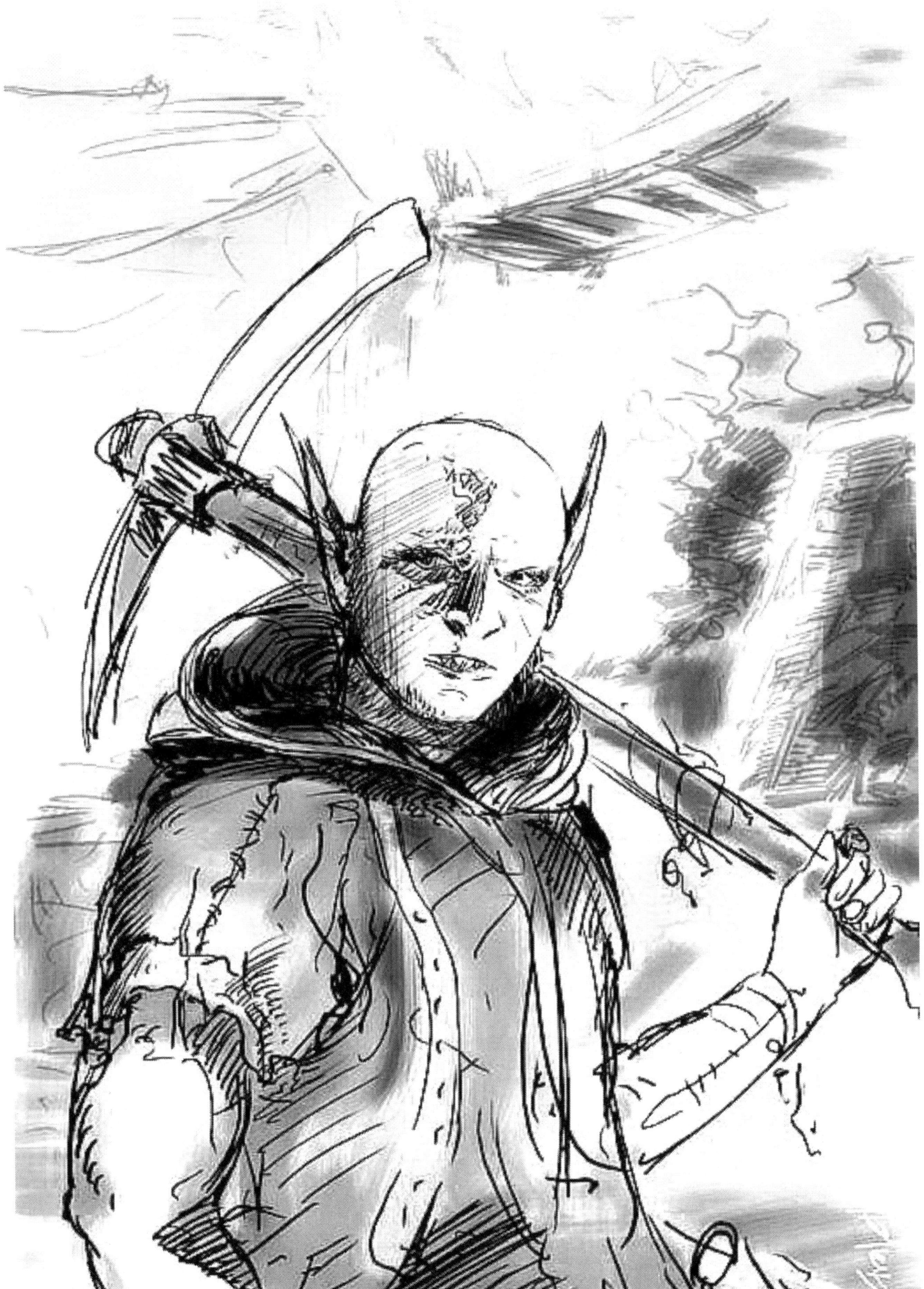

Multimedia Experience

Scan the QR codes below to watch the Book Trailers for The Coal Elf Chronicles!

"The Case of Crescent Fairway"

from *The Coal Elf Collection: The Lost Tales of the North Pole*

Maria DeVivo

Crescent's mother had been crying for days. She had tucked herself under her threadbare duvet, and woefully buried her face into her pillow. The muffled wails of lamentation that emitted from the downy cushion were hard to listen to. The entire Fairway family would stop in their tracks and cringe at each interval of hysterics. Mother was inconsolable, and rightfully so.

Cres's 9th Elfyear had come and gone without much fanfare. The entire week before, she waited with baited breath to receive her Life Job assignment letter, but then Mother took ill and… *oh who was she kidding?* She wasn't a stupid little elfling with lollipops and puppy dogs swirling around in her pretty little head. She knew the reason Mother was so grief-stricken was *because* of Cres's Life Job assignment. And that could only mean one thing… Cres's wildest dreams had finally come true.

Crescent Fairway of East Bank was going to be a Coal Elf!

Yes. She knew the stigma attached to the assignment was a devastating one for any family. Seven sisters before her had all been assigned a pleasant hand in life – a blessing from the Boss bestowed upon the Fairway family who had struggled to make ends meet in the heart of the City. They were a proud family of ten – Mother, Father, and eight girl elfchildren - who lived a simple and dignified life. No Nanny to help raise the girls, Mother Fairway kept the family together and maintained her part-time position as a Seamstress Elf at home.

Father Fairway worked odd jobs as a Handy Elf for all of East Bank. Often his work took him to the ritzier parts of the region where he would have to replace lightbulbs in the grand hallways of the Manors in Tir-La-Dunes, or give the wrought-iron entry gates a fresh coat of paint in Tir-La-Treals.

His work in Tir-La-Treals had familiarized him with the Skye family, and when Crescent was two elfyears old, the Skye's youngest daughter, Ember was sent to the Mines - not to be trained as an elfwife in West Valley, but to be a Coal Elf! This unprecedented event in current elf memory had put all families on notice and struck fear into every elfmother's heart. It became a cautionary tale for families of young girl elves, but Mother and Father Fairway had been so confident that the fates of their other seven daughters would prevail with their last, that they really didn't give the scenario a second thought.

Growing up, Cres had heard the stories of "Ember Skye - the only female Coal Elf in the Mines," and she was mystified by the legend. It was one that resonated deep in her soul. Ember was unique, Ember was different, Ember was the toughest chic in all the Pole – so strong that the Boss had handpicked her to toil in the dark and the dust. She *must* have special powers or something to be given that task! And for as long as she could remember, Cres idolized Ember because Cres wanted special powers, too. Cres had always felt like the outsider – at school, in the complex they lived in, and at home. There was a strangeness about her that set her apart from the other elflings her age – from the black curly hair that grew wild on top of her head, to her onyx colored eyes that looked like two perfect pieces of coal set perfectly in her long face. Cres's demeanor was unlike the others' too, as she often spent her time alone in her room or in the Town Square wandering the streets chasing the long-tailed corly creatures from the hidden alleyways. She didn't care about games like Brimmle Brummle, and she certainly couldn't stand to sing the song "The Mists of the North." But most of all, she struggled with the constant shadow of her seven sisters who were like a kettle of vultures looming over her, waiting for her weakest moments to swoop in for the kill.

Being a Coal Elf would really give them something to talk about! She thought joyfully to herself as she bounced back and forth on the curbside in the city. *Being a Coal Elf would show them just how powerful I am!* And she launched herself into the air and over a sewer grating in the street imagining herself parkour-ing off the cave walls in the Mines – the light from her work helmet glinting off the black rock, filling the deepest part of the cave with a glorious strobe effect.

It was a chilly summer evening in August. The snow drifted down in soft clumps, trying desperately to stick to each other as they hit the ground. Every Wednesday since the start of the summer, Crescent went corly hunting in the back alley of the Inn. She loved corlies. The little balls of fuzz scavenged the dumpsters and sewers in the city. Many elves found them to be a nuisance, like rats in the city streets, but Cres thought they were sweet, and cute. And because she was quick and stealthy herself, she was able to scoop them up, play with them for a bit, then relocate them to the woods. Cres had an agreement with Joona Snowshade, the tall, golden-haired elf who worked at the Inn in the Town Square. He oversaw the grounds and catered to the guests' every whim. One evening when summer had just begun, one of the cooks had told him there were strange noises coming from the dumpsters in the alley. Too afraid that it might be a Chyga or some other vicious creature, the cook insisted Joona take a look. Crescent had been lurking inside the dumpster chasing the alley corlies, and when Joona opened the canister and saw her jet-black eyes staring up at him, he had nearly jumped out of his skin! She giggled at his reaction, and he couldn't help but laugh back when he realized it was just a little girl looking up at him cradling three corlies in her arms.

"You scared my cook," he had said sternly as he reached in and lifted her up out of the container.

"I… I'm sorry," she had fidgeted nervously.

"Hmmm…" he pondered, scratching his chin. "You like corlies?"

Cres brought the fuzzy creatures closer to her chest and nodded her head fiercely.

"The thing about corlies though… they're bad for business. Tend to make a giant mess back here. Giant messes mean extra work. We just usually end up killing…"

A small squeal rose in Cres's throat. She tightened her grip on the clutch, and took a quick step back and away from Joona.

"However," he began with a smile, "I'll make you a deal. Being that you're so good at catching them, if you come by here once a week and catch as many of those critters as you can, I'll give you whatever sweet treat the baker is preparing in the kitchen for the next day."

So, for all of June and all of July, this was Crescent's job. Now, in mid-August, on the edge of her 9th Elfyear, her Life Job assignment still a lingering mystery, and her mother despondent and barely functioning, she took solace in her dumpster-diving responsibilities, and today was no different. Crescent would swing by the Inn, round up how many corlies as she could, get her oversized brownie or Santa Claus cookie and cup of hot cocoa, talk to Joona for a little bit, head out to the edge of the forest at Mon Valley, release the corlies, hop-skip-jump back to town, and saunter back home for the night. It was the perfect plan. It was her usual plan. For today wasn't any different than any other summer Wednesday.

But it was, because Crescent had thoughts of coal mining in her head, and she was a fraction distracted. So distracted, even, that she almost didn't notice the dark figure sitting at the window seat in the High Court Suite at the Inn…

Cres paused behind the practicing Choir Elves on the street before crossing over to the Inn. *No one ever rents that room! It's way too expensive!* she thought, but she continued to watch the figure watching the singers. There was a look of longing and pain on the elf's dirty face that Cres found so odd, so curious. There was a sadness in the elf's eyes that almost brought Cres to tears. And as the elf at the window stood up and tucked her dirty hair behind her pointed ears, it dawned on her that it was none other than Ember Skye!

Ember Skye! Coal Elf! Here! Aboveground!

She sprinted across the city street and burst through the front door of the Inn. Slarrett, the Inn Keeper, shot straight up from his chair behind the oak desk. "W… what is the meaning of this?" he declared.

His high-pitched voice made Crescent giggle on the inside for a moment. She raced to the desk and hugged the top of it with both her arms. "Ember?" she huffed breathlessly. "The Coal Elf. Is she here?"

Slarrett's eyes widened for a split second then narrowed. "You're Joona's little corly catcher, aren't you?" he said slyly, trying to change the subject.

"Please, sir. I need to see Ember. I saw her in the window. I need to speak to her."

Slarrett clicked his tongue against the roof of his mouth with a 'tsk-tsk' sound. "I'm afraid not, child. I have to protect the identity and privacy of *all* my guests." His emphasis on the word *'all'* made Cres cringe, although she couldn't really explain why.

"Please!" she begged. "At least let me see Joona!"

He shook his head. "I'm sorry, little lady. Joona is attending to our guests. Now, I suggest you either do the job you've been commissioned to do, or go home. Simple as that. I can't have you here upsetting my clients."

Desperation rose in Cres's body. She balled her fists and pounded them on the desk top. "You don't understand!" she pleaded.

"That is it!" Slarrett said raising his voice.

Cres put her hands defensively in the air. "Okay. Okay," she said and walked backward toward the door hoping maybe Joona or Ember would come down the narrow wooden staircase behind the desk.

"I don't want to see you here until next week!" Slarrett yelled.

Cres shuddered at the screech from his unusually high voice, turned around, and walked back home, deflated.

She was there. Ember was there! The whole week long, Crescent dwelled on all the questions she would have asked Ember. She dreamed of the conversations they would have had. She played every sentence, every syllable, and every made-up response over and over in her head. Ember was her hero! Her real-life hero! And she was literally one story away from her. If only she could have…

Even though she was different than her peer elflings, she still knew well enough to obey her elders. Be that as it may, Cres stayed away from the Inn the entire week. In fact, she didn't even go into the Town Square at all for fear of Slarrett's reprisal. The following Wednesday evening, on her distracted trek to the Inn, she nearly walked right into Joona as she entered the alley.

"Whoa, whoa, whoa, my friend! Watch where you're going!" he exclaimed in surprise.

"Oops! Sorry, Joona, I wasn't…"

"Paying attention? Child, you were practically on another planet! Everything okay, Miss Fairway?"

Cres clasped her hands behind her back and rocked back and forth on her heels. "Just a lot on my mind, I guess," she said as she shrugged her shoulders.

"Hmmm. I wonder what it could be?" he said unconvincingly.

She gave a small smile and raised her eyebrows.

"Slarrett told me what happened."

"What was she like? Did you talk to her? Is she okay? Is she totally cool? *And what was she doing Aboveground?"* she spat in rapid-fire fashion.

"Slow down, slow down!" he coaxed. "You can skip the corly hunt and I can have the chef make up some supper for us. I hear his summer squash pie is out of this world."

"No thank you," she said reluctantly (because summer squash pie was her favorite, and she had no idea if her Mother would be preparing anything for dinner tonight, and her tummy rumbled, and she was sad and excited at the same time, and…)

"Okay, I understand," he said gently.

"It's just that I really needed to talk to her. Joona, I got my Life Job and…" she blurted.

Joona's eyes widened with curiosity. "Oh? And?"

"I'm going to be a Coal Elf," she blurted again, nonchalantly.

"What do you mean?" he asked, confused.

Crescent breathed in deep, annoyed that she even had to get into this particular part of the story. Like, it's no big deal, or anything, but… "Yeah," she began. "Mother got my assignment a few weeks ago. She still hasn't told me officially, but I know. She's been all sick and stuff over it. So, yeah. Coal Elf. And I just had so much to ask Ember, and…"

"No you're not," he interrupted.

Cres's face twisted up. "Huh? What do *you* mean?"

"I hate to break this to ya, kiddo, but they're not taking anyone else in the Mines right now. Haven't you heard? They suspended apprenticeships in the Mines for this year. Maybe indefinitely. One of the head honchos down there apparently ripped up the Naughty List. They decided *no one* will get coal this year."

Crescent's face practically fell to the floor, and she froze in place. *No apprenticeships? No coal? What did this all mean? Where did she belong now?*

"Crescent? You okay, child?"

"Yeah. Yeah. Fine," she replied in a daze as she backed up from him. "I… I'm gonna go. I'll come back next week, if that's okay with you."

"No worries," he said with an understanding tone. "See you then."

Cres turned onto the main road and walked and walked and walked. There was a bite in the early evening air, and she jammed hands into her jacket pocket to keep them warm. Her mind felt fuzzy. It felt as if all her thoughts and dreams and hopes had swirled together in a snow cyclone and all at once dissipated onto the horizon and were melted by the last rays of the setting sun. She had planned. Plotted. Figured it all out. And now? Nothing? Surely, her parents would be ecstatic. She knew Mother would magically get well again, and all would go back to normal in the Fairway duplex. Her sisters might even be happy, too. Celebrations all around! Everyone would celebrate except for the one elf who had the most to gain from the prospect of being a Coal Elf – her!

And then it was dark - like, really dark. Like, there were no more street lights to guide the way in the Town Square. In fact, there weren't any more streets! Crescent gulped hard as a swarm of Graespurs flew overhead. She had wandered so far from town that she didn't recognize her surroundings at first, and a flash of panic took its grip on her because she realized no one knew where she was! She assumed that the tree line to her right was the outskirts of Mon Valley, so if she just turned around and retraced her footprints in the thin layer of snow on the ground, she would be alright, but then again it was dark. Scary dark. And crazy creatures roamed in the dark. Crazy creatures lying in wait for a juicy morsel of an elfling to stumble right into their jaws.

Then she saw hints of flickering lights and heard voices faintly carried on the eastern wind, and thought maybe if she flagged down an adult, they could help her get back home quickly and safely, so she continued with a hopeful heart toward the noises. And as she got closer to the voices, she realized exactly where she was! Transporter elves hurried to unload large packages from a snowcart, while Miner elves *heaved-and-hoed* them inside a large opening of a black rock cave. *The Mouth. The Mouth of the Cave! The Entrance to the Mines!* She picked up her pace to a steady trot.

But then the Transporters finished up, and sped away on their snowcart. The lights from the Miners' helmets disappeared one by one back into the cavern. All gone before Cres was within earshot! She hunched over, put her hands on her knees, and began to cry.

"Is somebody there?" a harsh voice broke through a blast of wind, and Cres perked up.

"I'm here!" she struggled to say, but her voice was strangled by the sting of the air.

An elf hobbled toward her. Gangly, gnarled, twisted – the shape was so completely bent up, she was surprised he was able to move. "Who are you?" he growled. "And what are you doing so far away from town?"

"I… I'm lost," she said through chattering teeth.

The strange elf pointed a crooked finger at her. "Lost? Or runaway?"

She paused, contemplating her answer. "A little of both, I guess." A strange smile swept across his emaciated face and he waved for her to come closer to him. "

Suppose you changed your mind about the running away part, eh? Suppose you're wanting some help to get home." He drummed his crooked finger on the tip of his chin.

She jogged closer. "Yes, sir. Both," she shivered. "My name is Crescent Fairway, and…"

"Fairway?" he grumbled. "A city elfling. Well, you just missed the boys going back into town, but…" he paused and bit his lower lip in contemplation. His sharp canine punctured the skin, and he quickly slurped up the red bubble of blood. "I do believe another delivery will be here soon. Why don't you come inside where it's warm? I was undecided about what to eat for supper, but you've given me a glorious idea! I can whip up some of my specialty stew while we wait."

An unsettled feeling simmered in Cres's stomach. "I… I don't know. Maybe I should just wait here."

"Nonsense! You feel that temperature dropping? You'll freeze out here. Besides, I'm a Master Elf. I have the perfect den for my apprentices with lots of toys and games to help pass the time if you don't feel like eating." He smiled a wicked smile.

"You're a Master Elf? I… I was told that the List was ripped up. There were to be no more apprentices in the Mines."

The elf's face twisted sideways. "And how do you know that?"

"I got my Life Job Assignment recently. I'm to be a Coal Elf. Well, not anymore," she kicked the snow around her and looked at the ground. "My friend Joona told me about what happened."

"And you *want* to be a Coal Elf?" he asked in disbelief.

Cres's eyes widened and she looked up at him, beaming. "Oh yes, sir! More than anything! I want to be just like the great Ember Skye, and…"

The elf took a step back, bent forward, and coughed wildly, interrupting Cres's train of thought.

"Are you okay, sir?"

"Yes, yes, fine, fine," he managed to say, catching his breath. "Come, Crescent Fairway," he said outstretching his arm to her. "I can show you first-hand what it's like to be an Apprentice in the Mines. I'll give you the grand tour of sorts. Who knows? Maybe we'll run into the *great* Ember Skye." He emphasized the word 'great' in a very peculiar way.

She reached for his hand, accepting his gift of a meal and a tour. "Okay," she said reluctantly. But it *was* late, and she *had* turned down Joona's summer squash pie, and she *was* ravenously hungry now.

"Excellent! I'm famished! Having you for supper is going to be a real nice treat!" he exclaimed, and he gripped her hand fiercely and jerked her arm hard that she stumbled over her footing in the snow. "My name is Corzakk, by the way," he hissed as they made their way into the Mouth.

The Coal Elf Chronicles
Available at:

BARNES & NOBLE BOOKSELLERS

BAM! BOOKS·A·MILLION

Walmart Save money. Live better.

audible an amazon company

amazon

DeVivo Maria DeVivo ★ Author

Visit www.mariadevivo.com

Like and Follow DeVivo on Facebook!
www.facebook.com/mariadevivoauthor

Follow DeVivo on Instagram!
@Mrs._DeVivo

Answer Keys

The Coal Elf
Crossword Puzzle

9	4	6	7	5	2	3	1	8
8	3	1	6	9	4	5	2	7
7	2	5	1	3	8	6	9	4
1	5	9	3	6	7	8	4	2
4	7	8	2	1	5	9	6	3
2	6	3	8	4	9	7	5	1
5	9	7	4	2	3	1	8	6
6	8	2	9	7	1	4	3	5
3	1	4	5	8	6	2	7	9

Aboveground Life

8	6	9	5	4	1	2	3	7
2	3	1	6	7	8	4	5	9
4	5	7	2	9	3	6	1	8
6	1	4	8	3	2	9	7	5
7	9	5	4	1	6	8	2	3
3	2	8	9	5	7	1	4	6
1	8	2	7	6	5	3	9	4
5	4	6	3	2	9	7	8	1
9	7	3	1	8	4	5	6	2

Answer to the Mystery Message:
EMBER LOVES TANNEN

Made in the USA
Columbia, SC
07 December 2022